Two Dogs and a Boy

Teresa Adele Bettino

Cover Photo
Michael Paust

Two Dogs and a Boy by Teresa Adele Bettino

Published in the United States of America by
Fer-Sher Publishing. www.fershERpublishing.com
P.O. Box 2762 Chester, Va 23831

Cover Photo: Michael Paust
Front Cover Design Michael Paust
Back Cover Design Sherry Ferrell

First printing

ISBN: 978-0-9742842-3-1

This story is dedicated to my son Joseph Green and my brother, Edward Thomas Bettino, Jr.

In memory of my companions Ladybug, Shadow and childhood dog, Chipper.

Books by the author:

The Adventures of Sugarbabe and Thunder

The Ten Commandments of a Welfare Worker

Degen and Me

The Cats of Hanover Juvenile Correctional Center

Unique Shadows

A Wicker Rocker

1

Like tumble weed blowing in the wind across a desert the hurricane winds and waves came boldly crashing onto Barnegat Inlet. Gales moved forcefully sending sand whipping wildly. Sand spun away from dunes forming circles into the night air. The Barnegat Lighthouse stood stoic. Winds blew around the lighthouse as roaring waves slapped the jetty. The force of the waves caused white foam to drift over boulders.

Anna-Maria DeVito, held me close. We stood facing the wind and watched as the angry surf pounded the jetty. Foam mixed with sea weed littered the shore line.

I was five years old at the time and remember this moment with my mother as if it were yesterday. Even today, I can hear the sound of the wind. I can recall the smell of sea salt. I can close my eyes and imagine sand stinging my face.

My mother always enjoyed a good storm, but didn't care for hurricanes. She always became excited to see rough surf.

Mom was raised on Long Beach Island, New Jersey. She was a woman of experience having lived through North Eastern storms or as some say, Nor'easter's and hurricanes.

Holding onto mom and putting my fingers into her long curly hair, I felt secure. I knew that she would hold on tight to me. As wind began to increase, mom decided to leave the jetties. She wanted to return to our house on 13th Street. Our yellow house, a small rancher, was a few blocks away.

"Eddie, let's get back to the car. Once we get home let's pop some pop-corn and watch a good movie. We can make a fire in the wood stove."

"Mom, how about if we watch the movie *Homeward Bound*? You remember, about the two dogs and the cat that are trying to find their family?"

Mom didn't answer. Instead, still holding me she began to run. My head bobbed up and down to her rhythm. She let me open the door and I swiftly climbed in. Mom then ran around to the driver's side and got into the car. Once inside she shivered; and proceeded to find a towel in the backseat of the car. I dried off just as she turned on the windshield wipers. Sand mixed with rain pelted our glass windshield.

As mom began to drive she said "I don't know Eddie; you've watched that same movie over and over again. I am tired of it. This is a good movie night. Maybe we can try one of the movies that we haven't seen. How about one that you received as a birthday present? Let me think it over, alright?"

As we talked, the wind began to blow harder. Rain, wind with sand lashed the windshield. It was difficult to see. Mom drove down Center Street. She huddled close to the steering wheel. I noticed that her eyes looked like little slits.

"Eddie, it is very hard for me to see. Make sure you are buckled-up. Even though we are almost home, you need to be sitting with your seat belt on."

"I am. Do you think that this is going to be a big storm?"

"Eddie, I think that this is going to be one of the worst storms that Long Beach Island has witnessed in a long time."

2

With gales as strong as 40 miles per hour, I could not help but notice that bushes and tree limbs were bending. Rain hitting the windshield made it very hard for us to see. Mom continued to drive, slowly, holding onto the steering wheel. She was sitting so forward that her stomach touched the wheel. Mom was shaking.

"Eddie, I am having a difficult time seeing. I am afraid that our car will go off the side of the road and get stuck onto the shoulder. If that happens we will be stuck. Buried deep with the sand our tires won't be able to get us out."

Just as mom was speaking she noticed something. She leaned further forward. I watched her and I leaned also. I squinted too. The windshield wipers continued back and forth. Sand continued with its mixture of rain and debris, which gathered on our windshield. In front of the car, mom noticed two black dots rolling. The black dots were crossing the street. The wind was pushing them. Mom slammed on the brakes. Our car skidded to the side. It stopped just short of the shoulder.

"Stay in the car," Mom commanded as she made a dash for it.

I leaned as close to the windshield as possible. My nose touching the window made fog form. I saw a slight image of mom kneeling and extending her arms. She picked something up. I could see her putting something under her drenched blue sweat shirt. She ran quickly, opened the car door, jumped in and squealed.

3

Life changed at that very moment. Years later, when I was in middle school, I asked my English teacher the definition of a *pivotal moment*. I had overhead mom talking on the phone to our neighbor, Mrs. Ryan. She was using the words pivotal moment.

"It means when your life will never be the same," she replied. "It can mean that you are taking a different road. That you have become aware. It means that you are growing and with growth comes change."

The driver's side of the car opened.

"Hold out your hands, palms up, Eddie."

"Why?"

"Dear God, Eddie, do as I say! You will not believe what I have found."

Hands held out. My palms up. Mom placed two black wet something in each of my palms. So small, that although their eyes were opened, they probably weighed about a couple of pounds. The furry wet, something was shaking in my hands.

"These are really young puppies. Eddie, please place them together on your lap. Pull your sweat shirt over them to give them warmth," Mom directed.

"Mom, what could have happened? Where is the pups' mom?"

"I don't know," Mom replied, as she began to drive intently.

As we approached the house, she stopped the car and began to give a series of orders.

"Eddie, give me the pups. I will give you the keys to the house. Use the front door key. Leave the door open. Once you get in go to the linen closet. Go and get the navy blue wool winter blanket. Eddie, on the count of three, get out of the car and run!"

"One-two-three!"

I heard her screaming over the storm. I opened the passenger side of the car and immediately felt the chilly, windy, rainy, air. I ran to the front porch, jumping the steps two at a time. Since we had not left the lights on, I found myself fumbling with the key. Finally, I was able to open the door.

I ran through the living room. I turned right at the hallway. I opened the linen closet door and found the navy blue wool blanket.

4

By the time I had completed my chores, mom was already out of the car and in the living room. I noticed that she had thrown all of the magazines out of the wicker basket. Scattered magazines were everywhere on the living room floor. I had to hop over several in order to give mom the blanket.

"Eddie, fold the blanket and place it inside of the basket," she commanded.

Mom then placed the puppies onto the blanket.

"I am going to look for the hot water bottle. Have you seen it lately, Eddie?"

I indicated no with a nod of my head. I proceeded to turn on the living room light in order to view the puppies. I could hear little shrilly noises. They were bunched up.

Mom returned with the water bottle. She had filled it with hot water. She removed the puppies from the basket and unfolded one layer of the blanket. She then wedged the hot water bottle in the unfolded spot and placed the remaining blanket over the bottle. She then placed the puppies on top of the hot water bottle and blanket. She had completed these tasks all with the use of one hand.

"Eddie, help me drag the standing antique lamp out of the guest bedroom. I want to place it over the basket to give the pups more light."

I took one end of the antique standing lamp and mom the other. Once in the living room, I plugged it in and mom turned it on.

Outside sand, wind and a mixture of rain was heard, beating on the roof and windows of our house. I prayed that we would not lose our electricity. I knew that this was going to be a long night.

5

With the excitement of two puppies, sitting on the sofa and the comfort of a warm fire in the wood burning stove, sleep came quickly. Mom covered me in an old quilt that her grandmother had made. She said that having a patched quilt reminded her of a book she had read a few years ago called, *Patches on the Same Quilt* by Becky Mushko. Mom said that we are all together in one universe and that we need to be kind to others, including animals. Animals and humans connect as patches do on a quilt.

As I slept I dreamt of mom and dad. Dad was in my bedroom reading to me. Dad tucked me into bed. We said our night time prayers. Memories of dad always made me sad. I missed him.

Awakened by noises of someone banging the kitchen cabinets, I got up off of the sofa quickly and padded into the kitchen. Mom was talking out loud saying "I just know that I put it in here!" She then found what she had been looking for. Mom had been looking for a container, of powdered baby formula. Mom would sometimes baby sit Mrs. Ryan's infant. She always had some in the cabinet.

After finding the formula, mom mixed it and poured it into two baby bottles. She had extra small nipples and placed one nipple on each bottle. With a quick twist she tightened the top of the bottle. The bottles were ready.

The pups had slept for about two hours and now were hungry. The sound of their crying was a high pitch. This sound I was not able to ignore.

"Eddie, please come here. I want to show you how to feed the puppies. You are going to have to be my helper. I can't feed two at one time."

"It doesn't look easy. The puppy you are holding is squirming and isn't opening his mouth."

"I know. This is so frustrating," Mom replied as she began pouring formula onto her finger.

Once the formula was on her pinky she opened the puppy's mouth. The puppy licked the formula. As he licked the formula mom placed the bottle into his mouth. He began to suck, much like an infant.

We followed the same method with the pointy-eared puppy. After both pups' filled their bellies, mom placed her pup on the floor onto some papers. I followed. They stumbled. The rump area of the pup wiggled and wobbled. Both pups used the bathroom and once their task was completed, we picked them up and held them. As we held them we gently stroked their soft fur. After a few minutes, they fell asleep in our hands. We gently lowered our pups to the wicker basket. We covered each and replaced the hot water bottle with some more warm water.

"Eddie, our puppies love this formula. As soon as the weather breaks, we need to take the pups to veterinarian, Dr. Taylor. Hopefully, Central Avenue in Harvey Cedars will not be flooded. We need to go all the way to Ship Bottom, as Dr. Taylor is not in Barnegat Light on Thursdays."

As the storm's force continued our lights flickered. Then the lights went out. Mom was prepared with candles and flashlights. My chore usually was to go outside to the wood pile. I would bring in wood for our stove. Mom decided against me going. She bundled up and when mom opened the back kitchen door, the rain and wind hit her. She fell back into the kitchen. Mom told me to watch for her from the kitchen window. When she came up the back steps carrying about 10 logs, I opened the door. Sweetie, our long-haired tabby came bounding into the house. She was drenched. Her hair was stuck to her skin. Sweetie stretched her back legs and I wiped her down with the kitchen towel. The cat reminded me of a wet rat.

With the kitchen door shut in the distance I could hear the wind howling. Garbage cans were banging together in the square stands that held them. I shivered at the thought of the storm. No electricity. Most likely Harvey Cedars would flood. There would be no way to get from Barnegat Light to Ship Bottom, just south of Harvey Cedars without a road. We would not be able to bring the pups to Dr. Taylor. At least we would have warmth from the wood stove and would be able to eat.

6

As the gales increased, mom and I made ourselves comfortable on the sofa. We sipped on hot apple cider that had been warmed by the wood stove. It was hard for me to imagine that we were using the wood stove this early in the year as it was the end of September, not November.

"Once the puppies awaken, we need to feed them again," Mom explained that it was just like having an infant. You feed, burp, change diapers and then the infant sleeps for awhile and the routine begins again. So, in between feedings we filled the bottles with formula.

As mom and I drank our cider, she gave me a Long Beach Island history lesson. Mom always loved reading history. She told me that the place where we lived, Barnegat Light had been named by a Dutch explorer. The word Barnegat means an inlet with breakers. Around the lighthouse the current is very strong. White caps are common along the jetties and no one is permitted to swim there. When storms come to this barrier island the storms can make a lot of damage. Mom spoke of the March, 1962 Nor' easter which was called "The Storm of the Century." Two storms were stalled over the Atlantic Ocean. As mom told this story, the storm continued to make its presence known. Shrubbery began to scratch at our living room windows.

Mom stopped talking and turned the portable radio on. Our local station was announcing that Central Avenue in Harvey Cedars was impassable. No one traveling from Barnegat Light would be able to leave the island.

"Mom, I don't think that Dr. Taylor will be opened tomorrow."

The whining and high pitched crying could be heard as the sand combined with rain pelted our roof and windows. We held our puppies; mine with pointed ears and mom's a bit plumper, with a long, thin tail.

Mom and I began to feed our pups and tell knock-knock jokes. We were hunkered in for the night. Secured from the storm we were contented. Then there were several loud knocks at the front door.

7

With street lights off the scene outside was scary. Garbage cans continued banging. Rain pelted the roof. Darkness lined 13th Street. We didn't want to look through the peep hole. We feared the worst.

Mom gave her pup to me. She walked to the front door cautiously, as she carried in her hand a hammer that she had acquired from the coffee table. The hammer had been sitting there for days. She was supposed to hang a picture. Mom held the hammer in her right hand behind her back. She peered through the peep hole. She opened the door. Our next door neighbor rushed inside.

Hope Lewis, a physical education teacher at Southern Regional High School, with a red hoody covering her straight blond hair was frantic. Her shoulders hunched and shaking she screamed that Jack was out at sea in this storm. As she entered the living room she took off her rain jacket and began to cry.

"Anna-Maria, I am really worried about this storm. Jack left this morning on *Fair Lady* to go fishing. He had scheduled this day about two months ago. He didn't want to cancel."

"Why in the world would anybody be out at sea in this weather?"

"I said the same thing. Jack said that the storm wasn't going to hit the island until around 5 PM. He said that he would be home around 3 PM. Jack said that this would give the guys plenty of time to fish."

"Who went with him?"

"Larry and Al," Mrs. Lewis said fretfully.

"I tried to reach him by cell phone. He isn't answering his phone. I am so worried. I think that something terrible has happened. I even called the Coast

Guard. I spoke with Captain Henry. He said that the waves were as high as 20 feet. Captain Henry said that he would not send any of his men out to sea until the storm settled."

"The walls in my house are closing in on me. Can I stay with you for awhile? I just don't want to be alone."

As Mrs. Lewis ended her sentence the screen to the back door blew away from the frame. It finally freed itself with a blast of wind.

With the wood stove blazing, Mrs. Lewis was able to see the pups. She had a puzzled look.

"Eddie, what are you holding?"

As I walked toward Mrs. Lewis, the pups began to squirm a bit and made a squeaking noise.

"Are they rats?"

"Guess again."

"Guinea Pigs?"

"Nope."

"Hope, they are two puppies that we found twirling across Center Street in this horrible storm," Mom said as she coaxed Mrs. Lewis to sit on the living room sofa.

The storm continued to rage as we handed Mrs. Lewis our pups. We told our story. She gently rubbed each puppy with her index finger. She then placed her cheek along the faces of each dog and rubbed. Still crying she kissed each of the pups.

8

Jack Lewis, tall and muscular, knew his way around Long Beach Island. He was raised on this island. His parents, Sam and Irene, loved the natural beauty of this 18 mile barrier island. About 4 miles from the mainland, Long Beach Island offered Irene the freedom to watch the migration of birds and Sam the freedom of the sea.

Growing up in Barnegat Light, the northern tip of this island offered Jack the opportunity to learn to fish and swim. His father owned a fishing boat. He taught Jack how to navigate their boat, *Fair Lady*. Sam earned a living taking tourists deep sea fishing. He had taught Jack how to respect the many moods of the ocean. Jack, enjoyed as a boy, baiting hooks and helping tourists bring in their catch.

On this September day, Jack woke up early. This had been a day planned with his boyhood friends, Larry Turner and Al Baylor. All were islanders. This was their annual event. To go to sea and fish once the tourists had left the island. It was their way of saying farewell to summer.

The men loved the smell of the sea and cries of gulls. The sea gulls would follow *Fair Lady* as it left the dock. At times their cries were ear piercing as gulls circled the boat calling. Al especially loved feeding birds. He would bring stale bread from home. As he threw pieces of bread into the air, gulls would dive, take a piece, and fly off.

After graduating from Southern Regional High School, Jack, Larry and Al attended The College of New Jersey. Jack majored in physical education; Larry, English and Al, history. All were teachers at the local high school located on the mainland.

Fifteenth Street dock was deserted when they arrived at 5:30 AM. The sun had not risen and the sky was starless. Winds were from the south. Larry brought some homemade biscuits and Al freshly brewed coffee. Feeling comfortable at sea, the three joked about the storm that would be arriving late in the afternoon. They would leave Beach Haven, near the southern tip of the island around noon and head home for Barnegat Light.

As the sun began to rise, the men left Barnegat Inlet heading for Harvey Cedars. They were aware of the strong tides at the tip of Barnegat Light and moved cautiously through the inlet and out to sea.

9

Mom showed Mrs. Lewis how to feed the pups. As Mrs. Lewis fed the pointed eared pup she began to talk about Jack.

"This isn't like Jack not to call. I have a feeling that something has happened to him. I keep thinking of the movie, *The Perfect Storm.*"

Mrs. Lewis began to cry again.

"Hope, I really think that there is a good explanation as to why Jack hasn't called. He could have left his cell phone in the car, or has it off."

I didn't like to see Mrs. Lewis crying. I wanted to cheer her so I started to play knock-knock jokes.

"What's black and white and read all over?"

"Playing a game of checkers?"

"Guess again."

"Oh, I don't know Eddie. I can't think. Just tell me the answer."

"It's the newspaper!" I laughed.

The intensity of this storm increased. As the intensity increased so did Mrs. Lewis's anxiety. She paced back and forth. She looked out of windows toward her house hoping to see Jack. She thought that she heard Jack calling her name.

Mom and I looked across the living room. Mom moved her shoulders showing me that she didn't know what else to do to help Mrs. Lewis. I felt the same way.

"Mrs. Lewis, can you read me a book?"

"What book would you like me to read to you, Eddie?"

"How about a Harry Potter book?"

"The Harry Potter books are about 800 pages. Eddie, how long do you think that this storm is going to be? I surely hope not 800 pages worth!"

Mrs. Lewis decided to play a game of checkers with me instead of reading. We also played Old Maid and told some more jokes. This seemed to keep her mind off things.

10

The men enjoyed fishing and catching up with some local gossip. The southern winds mixed with the warmth of the sun made this day exceptional.

As *Fair Lady* continued heading south, Jack stopped the boat to fish in Ship Bottom. There was a run on blue fish and the fish swam skimming the surface. Al joked that he didn't need a fish hook only a fish net to lean over the side and scoop up a bunch.

After about an hour, Jack headed for Beach Haven. Dolphins swam along *Fair Lady* flipping near the boat. Jack noted a change in wind. The wind suddenly shifted from the North. Waves began to become choppy.

Jack became concerned. Larry and Al hadn't noted the change in air. They were talking about The College of New Jersey's football and tennis teams. Larry had played football and Al tennis. They were active members of the college's alumni.

"I think I am going to turn *Fair Lady* around. The air has shifted and the waves are becoming choppy. I have noticed a few waves capping."

"My wife warned me about this storm. I didn't take her seriously," Al said as he started to gather some of the gear off of the deck.

"April said that we were due for a hurricane. I hadn't been listening to the weather since school started. Larry added.

As the minutes passed, rain began to pound the deck. Waves were cresting. Winds howled around the boat. The conditions were ominous.

Fair Lady inched her way home. Jack estimated that he was at Brighton Beach having just passed Haven Beach.

Larry reached inside of his right pant pocket. He was looking for his cell phone. Jack too. Both wanted to contact the Coast Guard.

"I must have forgotten to take my phone out of the charger. I left it on the kitchen counter," Larry said searching frantically in all of his pockets.

"Here is mine," Jack said flipping the phone and turning it on.

"The phone won't come on. It needs charging. I forgot to charge it last night. I didn't think to bring the charger for the car with me. I could have charged it as I drove to the dock this morning."

"Al, what about you?" Larry said.

"Mine is drying out. It fell out of my shirt pocket and into the dish water last night when I was helping Kathy with the dishes."

Feeling as though he could not breathe, Jack took a few deep breaths.

"I'm going to try and reach Captain Henry by CB radio."

All three looked at each other. Concern and fear were written on their faces.

Breathlessly, Jack turned on the CB and began making a distress call.

"I'm not getting a response."

"Try again," Al and Larry said simultaneously.

As Jack began to speak into the CB, a wave broke onto the deck of *Fair Lady.* She began to take on water.

11

As waves battered *Fair Lady*, Jack, Al and Larry decided to turn the boat straight out to sea hopeful that the waves would not pound her. Heading straight away from the shore line was their only hope for survival.

"Let's try the CB once more," Larry and Al suggested.

Jack walked swiftly across the cabin to the instruments and began screaming into the radio. "Calling for help. SOS. This is Jack Lewis, captain of *Fair Lady.* We are taking on water. Just south of Brighton Beach. Heading further out to sea. SOS."

Al and Larry positioned themselves on the bench attached to the cabin's wall. The table had turned over and was on the other side of the cabin.

Faintly amidst static the men heard a response from the radio. Then the crackling ended. The radio died.

As *Fair Lady* continued moving out to sea, a 10 foot wave broke onto her deck crashing loudly. The men attempted to look out of the porthole. Jack realized his tenuous situation. *Fair Lady* would not make it through the velocity of this storm. They were going to sink.

Jack opened the trunk. As life jackets were thrown to each man, lightning and thunder sounded near. The men, tears mixed with fear within their eyes, hugged and shook hands. They prayed to God for protection. Al had never learned to swim.

Jack opened the cabin door. He would be the last man off of his father's boat. As the next wave crashed onto the deck and the boat leaned to its side, Larry and Al jumped into the sea. Jack was swept off the deck by the intensity of the next wave.

12

At about 2 AM a car pulled into our driveway. Sheriff Brown, a thin tall man with a slight limp and beard knocked on our door. Mom again carried her trusty hammer to greet the knocker.

"I've been trying to locate Hope Lewis."

"She has been staying here. Hope is very upset as Jack, Al and Larry went fishing yesterday," Mom said, as she let Sheriff Brown, one of our neighbors into the house.

Standing in the doorway of the living room, Sheriff Brown quickly made a pool of water. Water dripped from his hat, which was guarded by plastic wrap.

Mrs. Lewis had heard the voice of Sheriff Brown. She padded into the living room, rubbing her swollen eyes.

"Hope, it is good to see you. I have been looking for you. We received a call from a ham operator, Matt King. He lives over by Sands Point Harbor. He received a faint distress call on his radio. We think that it was Jack calling for help."

"He went fishing with Al Baylor and Larry Turner. They were to return to Barnegat by 3 PM yesterday. They went fishing. I told him not to go. I told him about the storm coming. He said that he would be home long before the storm hit the island."

"This storm came up quickly. Jack, Al and Larry probably didn't realize what was happening when the winds suddenly shifted."

"Will the Coast Guard begin a search now?" Mom asked.

"Not until the winds and the waves lessen a bit."

13

As the waves swept the men into the Atlantic, each were set on different courses. Jack, Larry and Al were pushed down into the depths of the ocean. Spinning, not able to see where bubbles were going, they were unable to find the top. Not that it mattered. The waves and violence of the sea engulfed them.

At times they surfaced and screamed. No one was heard. The wind claimed their cries. Jack noticed a small light somewhere and attempted to head in the direction of the light. He attempted swimming to no avail. Waves crested above him. Some broke on him sending him plummeting under the water. He placed his arms straight in front of him after coming to the surface. The life preserver helped. He bobbed and after a few minutes a large wave crested where he was and carried him to shore. He was thrown from its wake. Landing on the beach violently he hit solid sand feeling as though all bones had splattered. He did not move.

Al, coming to the surface, was unsure of time and direction. Rain and wind stung his face causing him to wince. He called to his friends. He received no response. The wind's voice answered his calls. He prayed. Accepting fate, another wave hit him sending him to the depths of the Atlantic.

Larry bobbed like a cork. He thrashed in all directions. He tried hard to keep his mouth shut. Water entered and he felt that his lungs would burst. While floundering, a large piece of wood hit his stomach. Perhaps it was a portion of *Fair Lady.* He didn't care where the wood had come from. His thought was to cling to it and not lose it, as he felt that this wood would be his savior. Struggling to continue to hold onto it with both hands, he was hit by a large wave. The wave carried him to the shore. He landed with such intensity he felt the bones shatter in his legs. He collapsed on the beach.

14

Mrs. Lewis spent the latter part of the morning holding the pups and praying for the safety of the men. Mom at times would look at Hope and cry with her.

After a breakfast of scrambled eggs and ham cooked on the wood stove, Mrs. Lewis said her good-byes. Her plan was to return home and wait to hear from her husband.

"Hope, we have to wait to hear. There is nothing that you can do, but keep yourself busy and pray for Jack, Larry and Al's safety."

"I just don't know how much more I can take. Surely the Coast Guard by now is looking for them. It seems like the wind has shifted and the sky is starting to look blue."

The ladies said good-bye and by the time Mrs. Lewis closed the front door, the sun began peeking through the clouds.

I could not help but think of the men's fate.

Electricity was restored about 11 AM. Mom and I sat in front of the television watching breaking news. Jack Lewis, Larry Turner and Al Baylor's photos flashed before our eyes. Friends since childhood, all were reported missing.

Watching TV was interrupted by the whining of the pups.

"Mom, do you think that we should name the pups?"

"Yes, I think that we should. If no one claims them, I want them to be our family."

"I think Shadow is a good name for the chubby one. He is always following the pointed eared dog. He reminds me of the dog Shadow in the movie, *Homeward Bound.*"

"I know how much you love that movie, Eddie. Shadow it is."

"What name would you like for the pointed eared pup, Mom?"

"How about the name Lady? I think she may be female. She seems calmer and more relaxed than Shadow.

With Lady and Shadow named we whispered their names to them.

At around 6 PM, Mrs. Lewis returned.

"It has been a long day. I just couldn't stay home looking out of the living room window another minute. I hope that you don't mind my returning, Anna-Maria."

"We have just named the dogs," I said eagerly. I named the chubby one Shadow and mom named the pointed eared pup, Lady."

Mrs. Lewis smiled at us. She reached her hands out to us, wanting to hold both pups. She sat on the living room floor and held Lady and Shadow.

15

The bay and the ocean joined in Loveladies. Harvey Cedars lost several houses along the beach. Channel 10 news was showing aerial photos. I was hopeful that the news would not show the men again and planned to turn off the TV if I thought that Jack, Larry and Al would be on.

With the electricity on, Mom prepared my favorite, tomato soup and grilled cheese sandwiches with potato chips. After eating, we took turns feeding and petting Lady and Shadow. Mom and I were happy to give Mrs. Lewis something to do. It also gave us time off.

The pups looked to me as though they had gained a little weight. They ate every 2 hours and slept after eating. They loved to play with each other. Shadow was always trying to climb over Lady. They played with their mouths opened. Once tired, both would curl together in the basket.

"I bet that Shadow is a male," Mom stated as she took Shadow from Mrs. Lewis and gently placed him in the wicker basket. "He plays rough and is larger. I am hopeful that Lady is female."

"I guess that you will learn their sex when you take them for a check-up with Dr. Taylor," Hope said as she got up from the sofa and placed Lady along side of Shadow in their basket.

Having the pups to look after was a comfort to all.

About 9 PM the front door bell rang. Mom turned on the porch light and opened the door. It was Sheriff Brown. He was looking for Mrs. Lewis. Upon seeing the sheriff, Mrs. Lewis started to cry.

16

"**H**ow about some pop-corn and Pepsi? We can watch *Homeward Bound* as we feed, hold and play with Lady and Shadow."

"Ok," I replied, wishing that dad were with us.

As Sheriff Brown entered the living room, we felt his tension. I noted that his eyes were looking at the hard wood floor. His shoulders were dropped forward. He told us in one long breath that Jack had been found and had been admitted to Southern Ocean County Hospital. Larry had been found alive; Al was dead.

With this news, Mrs. Lewis fell to the floor, screaming and crying. Mom started crying and Sheriff Brown, realizing his error, quickly used his radio to contact Deputy Sarah Moore.

Deputy Moore arrived in a matter of minutes. She nurtured mom and Mrs. Lewis and explained that Jack had been found unconscious on the beach. Jack and Larry had been found about 50 yards from each other. Larry was semi-conscious and was being operated on. He had broken bones in both legs and cracked ribs.

As Deputy Moore softly spoke, she held Mrs. Lewis and Mom's hand.

"Al's body had been located on the beach in Ship Bottom. He had drowned. Kathy, Al's wife had been notified. Her parents were due to arrive shortly. They were on their way from Manahawkin. April is on her way to the hospital."

Deputy Moore who had attended Southern Regional High School with mom and Mrs. Lewis asked Mrs. Lewis if she wanted a ride over to the mainland. Hope shook her head no.

"I can drive myself. I will be ok. I need to be with Jack. This is awful."

Mom said her farewells to the deputy and Mrs. Lewis. Once the front door was shut, mom motioned me to come to her.

"Eddie, I need a big hug. So much has happened."

As I hugged mom, I started to cry. I missed daddy. I wanted dad. He would have been able to fix everything. Nothing had been right since he died.

Mom held me close, talking to me softly. She carried me to the sofa and turned on the TV.

17

Eddie's Grandparents, Michael Anthony DeVito and his young wife, Christina left Italy aboard a small trade vessel. Michael knew the captain of the ship and had built his brick house. The son of a brick layer, Michael was well known in Monterosso, Italy. Christina and Michael were from the same village. They were childhood sweethearts.

Christina loved sandy beaches and the sea. This coastline village offered her sun, sand, ocean and Michael.

Christina dreamed of living in America. She and Michael spoke of living in the United States. Michael would be able to find work as a bricklayer and Christina, an artist, wanted to open an art studio.

Michael, a tall handsome man, with olive skin and dark eyes, shared Christina's dreams. They were married at

18. A wedding along the beach of Cinque Terre as waves gently lapped, added to the uniqueness of this couple. Father De'Georgio performed the marriage vows. He had baptized both children. He had listened to their first confessions followed the next day with Christina and Michael's first Holy Communion.

Two weeks later, after saving money for two years, and with their parents' blessings they boarded Michael's friend's ship. Passage to America was uneventful and the ship docked at Ellis Island, New York.

Michael was able to locate work in Queens, New York as a construction worker. He became known as a fine bricklayer and was hired for side jobs around the boroughs of Manhattan.

Christina cleaned houses and dreamed of an art studio teaching skills of pottery design.

Michael and Christina took a course in English offered by the Queens High School. They quickly became friends with Jose and Rosa Gonzales. Jose and Rosa were from Mexico.

The couples spent time together. They shared their dreams of life in America. They would have each other over to their rented rooms to play cards and to enjoy food. Rosa was intent with learning English as she felt that this was her port hole to earning a better living and furthering her education. Rosa wanted to study to become a nurse.

Jose enjoyed working with his hands and was a good mechanic. He was hired to work in a shop, located on the Upper East Side of Manhattan. The foreman and Jose were from the same small town.

The couples practiced using their English skills on each other. They read children's books, went to the movies and listened to the radio.

"Do you like living in Queens?" Christina inquired one dreary day in February.

"I would like to live where I can farm."

"Why don't me and you, or is it you and I go to the library to look?"

The Queens Library not far from their rooms offered Rosa and Christina the opportunity to explore books about the United States. They decided not to live in the West, too far. They decided to focus their attention on the East coast as Christina wanted to live by the sea.

New Jersey, the garden state looked inviting.

18

Hope Lewis spent the night by her husband's side. She was relieved that Jack had been found alive. He had a high fever and infection from a wound he received on his leg. This high fever made him delirious. He called for Al and Larry. Hope knew that Jack did not know what had happened to his friends. Kathy was preparing funeral arrangements and April was a few rooms down the hallway with Larry.

Hope decided that she wanted to meet April in the hospital's cafeteria. She called Larry's room. Briefly speaking with April they decided to meet in one hour.

Hope kissed Jack's forehead and whispered to Jack that she would be right back. April left Larry's room.

April and Hope sat by the window in the cafeteria. Neither was hungry. They held hands across the table and cried.

"Larry doesn't know that Al is dead. Dr. Williams doesn't want me to tell him. He is concerned that Larry will become despondent."

"Jack is delirious with fever and calls to Larry and Al in despair. It must have been awful for the men to be caught at sea in the storm. I just can't even imagine."

"Have you heard from Kathy?"

"I called her to convey my condolences," Hope replied as she removed her hand from April's.

Hope looking down, not making eye contact with April, began to cry again.

"I am at a loss as to what to say, what to do. I haven't eaten or slept in 3 days."

"Al's funeral is scheduled for next Saturday. I won't tell Larry. I will attend for us."

"Jack is a seasoned sailor. I just don't understand how he got into this predicament. In one way I am angry at him for not taking my advice. I told him not to go."

"Al is to be buried in the family plot near Toms River."

"I know," Hope replied. Both began to cry.

19

Anna-Maria awakened to a sound in the kitchen. Sweetie was meowing for her morning meal. She enjoyed her daily 6 AM breakfast of canned Alpo and dry food.

Anna-Maria was unable to escape the bright September sun light beaming from the bedroom window. *I need to jump out of bed before I become depressed thinking of Michael."*

This self talk each morning had helped her endure the pain of losing her only true love. *How Michael could have been killed in Beirut? The father of my only child. Enlisted in National Guards. Too old for this.*

Lady, Shadow and Sweetie eagerly wanted her attention. Everyone enjoyed their morning meal. Anna-Maria enjoyed her caffeine. *A good cup of coffee gets me going.*

The pups since their visit with Dr. Taylor had been given a good bill of health. They were able to eat dried puppy chow mixed with meat and a little water. Shadow was gaining weight by leaps and bounds. Lady chewed her food and ate less. She would be a dog that needed to be coaxed to eat. Dr. Taylor had not received any phone calls about two missing pups. Resigned to the fact that her family had grown over night she smiled. Anna-Maria was thinking that this was a blessing. It would offer Eddie and her diversion from much sorrow.

When she turned around, Eddie was behind her. He was rubbing his eyes and holding his stuffed rabbit, Hop-Hop. The two were inseparable at night.

"Eddie, what is wrong?" Anna-Maria said as she picked Eddie up.

"I miss my daddy."

Hop-Hop fell to the floor, causing Eddie to cry harder. Anna-Maria leaned over and picked up the rabbit in one scoop.

I have to be strong for my son, she thought, carrying Eddie to the living room sofa.

"I miss daddy too."

Anna-Maria rocked her son and talked with him about daddy. She wanted Eddie to remember Michael.

After a few minutes, Eddie stopped crying. He was hungry. Cheerios with milk brightened his day.

After breakfast, Anna-Maria and Eddie watched *Homeward Bound* again for the hundredth time.

20

Mr. Baylor's funeral took place in a wooded family plot. Southwest breezes provided a pleasant feeling to this depressing day. Since Mr. Baylor had served in the military, his wife requested a military funeral.

Mom and I held hands as the minister said prayers. Mr. Baylor's parents and Mrs. Baylor sat along side of his casket. They wept. Mom held me close and she cried. I felt very sad.

Reverend Goode spoke of Mr. Baylor's life. He loved hiking in the Pine Barrens and loved playing sports. He especially enjoyed fishing with his friends, Jack and Larry.

A veteran, Mr. Baylor respected and loved America. Reverend Goode said that Mr. Baylor was honored that he had had the opportunity to serve in the

Army. Freedom, Mr. Baylor felt was essential for all individuals.

As Reverend Goode spoke, I watched as the American flag flapped over the casket, showing dark wood. The warm breeze and cloudless sky blended with the brilliance of fall trees and the flag's colors of red, white and blue.

After Reverend Goode finished speaking, soldiers methodically folded our American flag. It was folded into a small triangle shape. One soldier handed the flag to Mrs. Baylor. Taps played in the background as the wind, once warm suddenly shifted from the North. A chill ran up my spine and I wanted mom to pick me up and to hold me.

We held hands and said the Lord's Prayer as Taps continued. Mom and Hope Lewis cried. I cried too and mom looked down and picked me up. She hugged me and her tears dripped onto my head and face.

Once the music ended, everyone began to leave. When I looked back, Mrs. Baylor was the only one left. She remained seated. Her head was down and her tears dripped onto her husband's flag.

When mom and I were in our car heading back to Barnegat Light, we didn't say many words. Mom said that she felt sad. I felt sick to my stomach. I told mom that I had a stomach ache. I missed daddy. Why did he die? Perhaps daddy and Mr. Baylor would meet in heaven.

Sometimes, I think that the passage of time has helped to lessen the knot in my stomach when I feel sad. I can remember mom saying something like, that life pushes you forward whether you want to go or not. I think this is the best way that I can explain the day of Mr. Baylor's funeral. Mom, Hope Lewis and I were pushed forward.

The north wind pushed us away from the grave site. The north wind pushed the car back to the island. The north wind moved day into night.

When mom and I arrived home we played with our pups. They brought us much joy and laughter. We played a game of Old Maids and I played ball with Lady and Shadow. Tired, after a long day, the pups, mom and I went to bed.

I was hopeful that tomorrow the north wind would cease. I didn't want it pushing me any more. I wanted time to stop so that I could think of dad as I never wanted to forget my daddy.

21

Queens Library offered the solution. Rosa and Christina would talk with their husbands about moving. Rosa would show Jose pictures of New Jersey and Christina would borrow the book to show Michael. Rosa saw gardens, Christina the Atlantic.

The couples planned a trip to New Jersey. They would travel to Toms River. Michael had a side job, building a brick wall. Michael's friend had a car and was willing to drive.

The thought of traveling outside of Queens was exciting. Rosa and Christina cooked so that they would have food during their travels. Christina baked chicken and Rosa made a bean and rice dish. Dessert would be a chocolate cake.

Leaving New York and traveling to South Jersey took a few hours. Rosa eyed the land. There was much land for gardening. Christina's thoughts were of living near the ocean.

The driver Larry Lavine had a cousin living in Toms River. His cousin said that they could spend the night. Larry knew how to reach his cousin's house. They stopped and were greeted by Allen and Ann Horowitz. Jose, Rosa and Christina stayed, as Larry left with Michael so that Michael would be able to meet Jim Raney. Jim had hired Michael to build a brick walkway.

Michael and Jim discussed the job and Jim mentioned several side jobs needed on an island not far from Toms River. He said that Michael would be able to live free in Jim's summer house. The side jobs would last until the end of June. Michael and Jim discussed salary and Michael realized that he could earn more money and live for free for 4 months. They agreed. Jim would loan Michael a car.

The following morning Larry drove the Gonzales and De'Vitos' to Long Beach Island. Jim's house was on the ocean side. He wasn't far from Barnegat Lighthouse. Christina instantly fell in love. The island was remote. A small bridge connected Long Beach Island to the mainland.

Larry Lavine returned the happy couples to Queens. Jose had located a job at a nearby auto mechanic shop. Rosa would clean houses and they would remain for a few weeks in New York. They planned to relocate to Toms River in the very near future as job prospects were good. Michael would work on Long Beach Island and Christina would help Michael at the job site.

When Michael returned to New York, he took his test for his license. He passed and was able to drive. Larry drove Michael and Christina, after they had packed what little possessions that they owned, to Jim's house.

Larry returned to Queens.

With the ability to drive and have a car, the happy couple explored this barrier island. The only road was narrow and at times sand covered the road making it difficult to drive. Michael drove to the southern tip and they explored this area of the island. Christina still loved Barnegat Light, where dunes seemed to reach the sky.

Christina frequently spent her time off sketching scenes of ocean, birds and dunes. She was interested in the sunken ship that wrecked on 12th Street, which was visible from the shore. During low tide she felt as though she would be able to walk to the ship, however; the water was too rough and deep.

When June arrived, Christina and Michael did not desire to leave. Jim hired Michael as a partner in his construction business. Michael would remain on the island and build. There was interest in investing in land on the island as business was booming.

Years went by and Christina and Michael built their house. The home located on the ocean side of 12th street, a few doors away from Jim's home offered Christina and Michael a sense of accomplishment. Michael built an art studio for his wife facing the dunes. The east window offered views of the sun rising with the beauty of sea grass, dunes and sky. Christina advertised art lessons by placing sketches of ocean views in markets and shops. She taught at their house.

22

As the pups grew, I grew too. I enjoyed playing games with Lady and Shadow as they were my pals. During the winter, there were not a lot of kids my age around Barnegat Light. In summer, I readily made friends with those families renting summer cottages.

Lady loved to sleep on the sofa and watch Saturday morning cartoons with me. Shadow enjoyed the low bunk bed in my bedroom. When I was in my bunk above him, I would tie a string to a bone and swing the bone back and forth in front of his nose as he slept. Of course, with his keen sense of smell, one sniff and he was intent on eating the bone.

Lady and Shadow were inseparable. They dug holes in the back yard and tore mom's laundry from the clothes line. At times they would take a sheet and play tug-of-war. After playing, they would take a snooze in the sun together, side by side.

Shadow loved swimming and enjoyed the ocean. Lady did not like the water and stood at the edge not wanting to get her feet wet. She would watch us swimming and coming back to shore, only to run out again. Lady, was my protector, and Shadow my playmate.

Teaching Shadow to fetch was easy. As a retriever, he always had something in his mouth to greet mom and me especially when we returned home. My best friends were my pups.

I enjoyed playing hide and seek with the pups. I would hide in a garbage can and wait for the pups to sniff around the property to find me. Shadow usually was first to locate me.

At night, when I was taking my bath, I would call Shadow into the bathroom. He would jump into the tub and splash around with me. Lady sat watching us.

At times she would bark, which would alert mom.

Mom would come into the bathroom and scold Shadow for jumping into the tub.

At bedtime, mom would read to me. The pups would climb onto the lower bunk and snuggle. I would be on top. We listened to stories. Once asleep mom turned off the light and shut the door.

Sweetie at times would join me sleeping on the top bunk. The pups and Sweetie were friends too. They were often seen sleeping on mom's bed together.

23

At age 51, Christina and Michael were blessed with a baby boy. The happy couple named their welcomed child, Michael Anthony DeVito, Jr. They considered Mike a miracle.

Anna-Maria Pinera met Michael Anthony DeVito, Jr. in kindergarten. Her parents lived in Ship Bottom, a few miles south of Barnegat Light. Since they lived on an island, all kids attended the same elementary school.

Anna-Maria had the curliest hair that Mike had ever seen. It was black, long and wiry. Mike sat behind Anna-Maria. He loved to play with her hair. He would put pencils in her long hair. Anna-Maria hated Mike.

In their junior year of high school, Anna-Maria found herself in the same English class as Mike. She sat in front of him. Mike no longer played with Anna-

Maria's hair. He thought that she was the most beautiful woman in the world. He asked Anna-Maria to his junior prom and she accepted.

They fell in love. They were high school sweet hearts and married after high school. Both attended college at Glassboro State. Anna-Maria majoring in English and Mike, in physical education. During the summers he helped his father with construction and Anna-Maria worked for the department of recreation and parks, running a summer day camp. They saved their money and after graduating from college located teaching positions on the mainland, in Manahawkin.

Edward Michael DeVito nick named "Eddie" was born twelve years later. He was loved by his grandparents and having been the first grandchild born on both sides of this Italian family, he was pampered.

Mike joined National Guards to add a little extra income for his family. He didn't think it a big deal as most of his friends were enlisted with the guards. It didn't become an issue until the United States became involved with Iraq. Mike wasn't one to watch the news, but soon discovered that members of the guard would be deployed to Iraq. He was one.

My grandparents, my mom and I drove to Manahawkin to say good-bye to Dad. Mom and Nana wept throughout our drive to the mainland. This was not in the plan. I needed daddy. How would mom and I manage without dad?

"Don't worry Eddie; daddy will only be gone about 6 months."

Dad was killed within one month of deployment. He was a victim of a car bombing. His body returned to mom in a wooden casket. Dad was later cremated and we threw his ashes into Barnegat Inlet.

24

I love fishing. Mom said that I am a lot like dad. He liked to fish, swim and surf on 12th Street beach. Lady and Shadow loved fishing too. Shadow especially as he enjoyed watching the sea gulls. He also liked playing with crabs.

I had a crab cage and would hang it on the side of the pier. Within minutes I would trap a couple of crabs and open the cage letting them scatter onto the dock. Lady would bark and back up. Shadow would try and place his foot on a crab. It was not unusual for crabs to scramble off of the dock with Shadow following into the bay. Shadow would swim to shore, shake and we would catch some more crabs.

One day, I threw my fishing line out. There was a minnow at the end of the hook. As I threw, a sea gull swooped and grabbed the minnow taking the line. My fishing pole was snatched from my hands and went with the gull. Shadow tried to follow the bird and pole. He turned back and came to shore. Mr. Banks, sitting in a row boat, rowed to the pole and cut the line before my fishing pole sank. He rowed to the dock and gave it back.

"Eddie, that sure was something to see. I wish that I had a video camera as I could have entered it on *America's Funniest Home Videos*. You should have seen your face!" Mr. Banks said and held his stomach as he laughed.

I didn't feel like laughing. I was embarrassed by what had happened. I was supposed to be a good fisherman. I was returning home with a smelly dog and no fish.

When I entered high school, the pups were beginning to slow down. They didn't want to come to the beach to watch me surf anymore. Most of their days were spent sleeping in the sun in the yard. Mom said that they were getting old and we needed to respect that.

"We get old Eddie. We are born and live our lives. The process of life is to die."

"I know."

25

When I was a freshman in college I received a frantic phone call from mom. She wanted me to come home from The College of New Jersey as soon as possible as Lady and Shadow were sick.

Driving the distance about 3 hours, I did a lot of thinking. I recalled when mom had found the pups and remembered the storm. I hadn't thought about Jack and Hope Lewis, Larry Turner and Al Baylor in a long time. I hadn't thought about Mr. Baylor's death. I hadn't thought of fate. Why is it so that some of us die early and some of us live long lives?

I remembered mom talking about animals and humans needing to share and be a part of a quilt. I believe this to be true. This is true for people throughout the world. This is true for animals throughout the world also. We are here together.

My dogs taught me to care for others and to give friendship and love to those in need. The night that mom found Lady and Shadow they needed to be loved and cared for. Mom and I needed to give love and to care for. We were lost without dad as our friend. Lady always, my protector and Shadow, my friend, enabled me to feel a sense of family that had been lost when dad died.

Dr. Taylor greeted me at the house when I arrived. Mom was crying as Lady was unable to stand. The arthritis was too much and she was in pain. Shadow had been diagnosed with a cancerous tumor in his throat and he was unable to eat. It was time for my friends to pass.

Mom and I held our pups together as we sat on the living room floor. Tears flooded the area as we spoke to our pups. Our love for them was immense.

About one week later, I returned to Long Beach Island. Mom and I stood in front of Barnegat Lighthouse. The waves lapped onto the jetty. The wind was faintly touching our faces. The sunny blue sky shone brightly over the horizon. Our pups had been cremated together. One urn held Lady and Shadow's ashes. Mom and I threw their ashes into Barnegat Inlet. This I considered a pivotal moment. Our lives would never be the same without our friends.

After the last of the ashes were scattered into Barnegat Inlet, mom and I held hands. We said a prayer for our pups. We said our final good-bye.

Author's son, Joseph with childhood companions, Ladybug and Shadow

Two Dogs and a Boy By Teresa Adele Bettino

www.ingramcontent.com/pod-product-compliance
Lightning Source LLC
LaVergne TN
LVHW020654100826
845148LV00012B/2485

* 9 7 8 0 9 7 4 2 8 4 2 3 1 *